For Gma, Gpa, and all of their webby guests

Bloomsbury Publishing, London, Oxford, New York, New Delhi and Sydney

First published in Great Britain in October 2018 by Bloomsbury Publishing Plc
50 Bedford Square, London WC1B 3DP

First published in the USA in June 2018 by Bloomsbury Children's Books
1385 Broadway, New York, New York 10018

www.bloomsbury.com

BLOOMSBURY is a registered trademark of Bloomsbury Publishing Plc

A CIP catalogue record of this book is available from the British Library

ISBN 978 1 5266 0624 2

All papers used by Bloomsbury Publishing are natural, recyclable products made
from wood grown in well-managed forests. The manufacturing processes
conform to the environmental regulations of the country of origin

Printed and bound in China by Leo Paper Products, Heshan, Guangdong

1 3 5 7 9 10 8 6 4 2

Bear's Scare

JACOB GRANT

BLOOMSBURY
CHILDREN'S BOOKS
LONDON OXFORD NEW YORK NEW DELHI SYDNEY

Bear was sure of many things.

He was sure that his house was clean.
He was sure that his rooms were tidy.
He was certainly sure that he took very
good care of everything inside.

There was one thing Bear loved to care for most of all. A small stuffed friend, named Henry.

They were always together.

Each day Bear and Henry cleaned the house high and low. They cleaned inside and out. It was on such a day that Bear found something odd.

“That’s funny,” said Bear. “I am sure
I did not leave any books out.”

When Bear looked closer,
he saw something not funny at all.

Bear tried to keep calm, but the more he searched, the more messy webs he found.

"Henry, we have a spider problem," said Bear.

"I am sure the spider is covering our home
with more sticky webs."

“I am sure the spider is making a giant mess with its many legs.”

“I am certainly sure the spider is nothing like us,” said Bear.

“Henry, we must find this messy guest.”

Bear and Henry searched high and low.
They searched inside and out.

But they did not find any spiders.

“This spider is extra sneaky, but it cannot hide from us!” said Bear.

He sprang up to continue the search, when something terrible happened.

Bear lay there for some time.

“My poor friend. I really never meant to make such a mess.”

Once again, Bear searched high and low.
He searched inside and out.

He had to find a way to help his friend.

When Bear returned he could not believe what he saw.

His dear Henry was good as new.

There among the books, Bear found
something he never expected.

He did not mind the spider's sticky webs.
He did not mind the spider's many legs.

"I certainly do not mind sharing my home with one more friend."

And that was something Bear could be sure of.